Kids love reading
Choose Your Own Adventure®!

"I loved the twists and turns of
the different endings."
Karianne Morehouse, age 12

"This is a flashlight-under-your-covers book
to read at night. It's exciting, thrilling
and fun all at the same time."
Walker Curtis, age 11

"I like the places the author chose to put the choices.
It really makes it hard to put down the
book because it's like you're in the story."
Haley Behn, age 11

"It's really cool how you get to choose the end!
It made the book really fun to read."
Josh Farber, age 12

Watch for these titles coming up in the
Choose Your Own Adventure® series.

Ask your bookseller for books you have missed
or visit us at cyoa.com to learn more.

ESCAPE

BY R. A. MONTGOMERY

ILLUSTRATED BY JASON MILLET
COVER ILLUSTRATED BY SITTISAN SUNDARAVEJ
& KRIANGSAK THONGMOON

CHOOSE YOUR OWN ADVENTURE® CLASSICS
A DIVISION OF

CHOOSECO
WAITSFIELD, VERMONT

Illustrated by: Jason Millet
Cover illustrated by: Sittisan Sundaravej & Kriangsak Thongmoon
Book design: Stacey Boyd, Big Eyedea Visual Design
Chooseco dragon logos designed by: Suzanne Nugent

For information regarding permission, write to:

CHOOSECO

P.O. Box 46
Waitsfield, Vermont 05673
www.cyoa.com

ISBN 10 1-933390-48-4
ISBN 13 978-1-933390-48-2

Published simultaneously in the United States and Canada

Printed in the United States

0 9 8 7 6 5 4

To Anson & Ramsey

With thanks to Julius Goodman
And to my good friend Bill Coffin

BEWARE and WARNING!

This book is different from other books.

You and YOU ALONE are in charge of what happens in this story.

There are dangers, choices, adventures and consequences. YOU must use all of your numerous talents and much of your enormous intelligence. The wrong decision could end in disaster—even death. But, don't despair. At anytime, YOU can go back and make another choice, alter the path of your story, and change its result.

The year is 2045 and despite your young age, you are returning from a secret spy mission to Dorado, the repressive police state that now occupies New Mexico, Arizona and Texas. You and your group must make it safely back home to Turtalia in the north. You have succeeded in acquiring secret plans for the Doradan invasion of Turtalia. Getting this information into the hands of Turtalian leaders will save thousands of lives. But the journey north to the city known as Denver is long and treacherous. And it difficult to know who you can trust to help get you there...

You are one of the leaders of a spy mission operating in the country of Dorado. You have just broken out of a maximum security prison run by the Doradan Secret Police. Your escape has only just begun.

Now you and your group must make it home to safety in Turtalia, which is more than a thousand miles away over semi-desert land and vast mountains.

The year is 2045. A combination of civil wars and foreign attacks has split the United States into three hostile political areas—Dorado, Rebellium, and Turtalia.

Dorado is a repressive police state. It follows only the rule of force, not law, and has designs on the territory of its neighbors. The Doradan Secret Police are feared throughout the continent.

Turn to page 3.

The second region, Rebellium, occupies all territory east of the Mississippi. It is a haphazard collection of minor city-states. They are disorganized and offer no real help in the struggle with Dorado.

Turtalia, which you are trying to reach, is made up of the mountain states north of Arizona as well as the northern plains states extending into Canada.

The capital of Turtalia is Denver. Turtalia is a democracy run by elected representatives and governed by a panel of five. It is also your home.

Your father is one of the panel of five. He was opposed when you volunteered to go on a spy mission into Dorado, but you went anyway. You were sure that you, and only you, could get the plans for the Doradan invasion of Turtalia—and you did get them.

The Doradan Secret Police arrested you, but fortunately they never suspected that you had learned their invasion plans. Your escape from their prison was due to luck more than to good planning.

Turn to page 4.

4

Right now you are hiding in a barn on a deserted ranch. You're about seven miles north of what used to be called Gallup, New Mexico. Three other people are with you. The most important—except for you, of course—is a thirty-year-old woman who is the leader of the resistance in Dorado. Her name is Mimla. There is a large price on her head. She has to get out!

With Mimla is Matt. He's in his early thirties, and it is his responsibility to get her safely out of Dorado.

The third person is a computer specialist named Haven—a silent, nervous man who peers at the world through thick glasses. He is needed in Turtalia to help break Doradan computer codes.

Your father, acting through the resistance organization in Dorado, has arranged an escape flight for the four of you. This morning you wait for a Windmaster twin-engine motor-glider to swoop out of the clouds and pick you up.

Turn to page 6.

6

You've been waiting for several hours. The plane is now half an hour late. Matt wants to leave.

"I think we should get out of here and head back to town. I don't want to get caught out here," he explains.

You look at the clouds, then at the desert.

"I don't know," you say finally. "We're in a pretty good spot right here. We can see anyone coming for quite a distance. I know Bill, the pilot, he's reliable. He'll get here! I think we can wait another half an hour."

"They're closing in on us," Matt says tensely. "I can feel it."

There is no sign of the Secret Police on the horizon. But you know they could appear at any moment.

If you decide to follow Matt's suggestion and return to town, turn to page 10.

If you decide to wait another half hour for the plane, turn to page 15.

You jump to your feet. It's a good thing you can wake up quickly. You and Matt join the others outside. The motor-glider has started its engines for the final approach.

You admire the slim craft as it swoops down. The Windmaster is a perfect combination: designed in 2012 to be a full-performance glider and power plane, it uses almost no gas once it is airborne. You wouldn't mind having a Windmaster of your own.

The plane is close to the ground, ready to land. You can see Bill at the controls and the Doradan military markings that have been added to the tail as camouflage. Then the plane bobbles, one wing almost catching the ground. Bill straightens it out and touches down. You wonder what that was—crosswind, maybe?

Bill taxis close, swings around to be in position for takeoff, and stops, engines idling. The four of you grab your stuff and run to the door.

You clamber aboard and throw your gear aft. You'll secure it later. You've got to take off quickly in case the plane was spotted.

"All set, Bill!" you shout.

There's no answer from the cockpit. You look at Matt questioningly. He shrugs his shoulders. You run into the cockpit. Bill is slumped over the wheel. He's not breathing!

Turn to page 13.

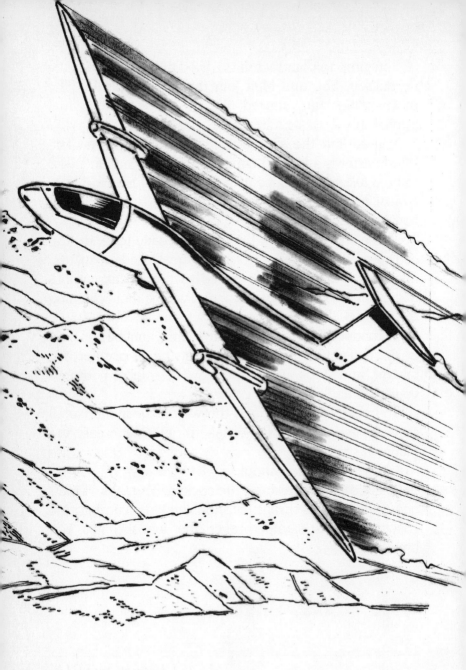

"Welcome aboard, copilot," you say to Matt.

Grinning ear to ear, Matt salutes you. "At your service, pilot," he answers.

While you buckle into the pilot's seat, Matt goes aft to make sure that Mimla and Haven are all set for takeoff. They have made a makeshift bed for Bill and are trying to keep him comfortable. When Matt returns, you quickly run through the instruments and switches with him: altimeter, variometer, fuel gauges, tachometers, engine temperature, throttle controls, engine heater switches, and so on.

Everything is ready. You roll the plane to the end of the strip. Your heart pounds in your chest, but otherwise you feel calm and capable.

Once more you scan the control panel. Then you adjust the throttles. The plane begins rolling down the sandy desert. At the right moment you pull the control column back and you're airborne. You did it!

The altimeter spins rapidly as your Windmaster climbs out and heads toward the Sangre de Cristo Mountains. You pass through 15,000 feet, then 16,000. Finally you top out at 17,000 feet. All around you are towering cumulus clouds bulging with moisture. You know that some of them hide violent turbulence that could easily rip the wings from the plane.

Turn to page 17.

Maybe Matt is right. Maybe waiting for another half hour is too risky.

"OK! Let's get out of here," you tell him. "No telling when that plane will get here—look at those clouds. But where do we go when we get back to town, Matt?"

Matt gathers up two canvas sacks filled with personal belongings and several Doradan military manuals and maps that Mimla and Haven have stolen. He shoulders the packs, and then looks at the clouds for a few seconds.

"Not much of a choice," Matt says. "Back to my friend Julio's place. It's so close to the Secret Police headquarters that they'll never look for us there."

You nod in agreement, but in the bottom of your stomach you feel knots of fear at the very mention of the Doradan Secret Police. You'd like to be as far away from them as possible.

Later that afternoon, you all wait in the living room of Julio's thick-walled adobe house in the middle of downtown Albuquerque. From the front window you can see the stark outline of the modern glass-and-concrete building that is Doradan Secret Police head-quarters. Two armed men wearing desert camouflage uniforms stand with their feet apart, laser guns at the ready, surveying every person who passes by.

Turn to page 12.

12

Mimla sits in the far corner of the living room, listening intently to a shortwave radio. She looks up.

"The plane is down. The Doradans got it over Santa Fe. I hope the pilot doesn't know much. Maybe he's dead anyway."

Haven cringes in another corner, paler than ever. Matt clenches his fist.

"We have to get out," you tell them. "They'll be on to us before you know it. I've got to get the Doradan invasion plans back to Denver. Anybody got any ideas?"

Mimla rises and walks to the center of the room. She looks at each one of you.

"I think we should split up. I'll go with you," she says, gazing in your direction. "OK?"

Matt disagrees. "We've got to stick together. We can try to get out of town on foot."

"It's a long way back to Denver," Mimla remarks.

If you agree to split up and leave with Mimla, turn to page 20.

If you argue for staying together, turn to page 21.

"Matt!" you shout.

He races into the cockpit after you.

"Help me with Bill!" Quickly you undo Bill's seat belts and ease him out of the seat. He is pale. You check his pulse: almost nothing.

"What's the matter with him?" Matt asks.

"Heart attack, I think. He looks bad."

"Oh, no," Matt groans. "Now what do we do?"

"Well, I have some glider training, and I've flown in one of these before," you say. "I think I can fly it out of here."

"I've had a little power-flight training," says Matt. "It sounds like we could do it. But it's risky. Maybe we should forget the plane and use the truck to drive out of here the easy way—on the ground."

Matt grins at you. You start to smile back, but you're interrupted by Mimla's shout from the cabin behind you.

"Somebody's coming!"

You look out from the cockpit and spot a telltale dust cloud.

"They're still a ways off," Matt says. "Doradan troops, probably. We'd better decide what to do—and quickly!"

If you decide to try your skill at piloting the Windmaster and fly out, turn to page 9.

If you decide to take the truck and risk getting caught on the ground, turn to page 16.

"It's too soon to give up. Let's wait for the plane," you tell the others. "Bill probably ran into bad weather. Anything can happen up there."

Mimla nods. She looks calm and ready for anything. But Haven, who's sitting in a corner of the barn, looks ready to jump out of his skin. He keeps pulling folded computer readouts from his pocket, fumbling through them, and then stuffing them back into his pocket.

You sit down in a comfortable spot in the hay. The sun is shining through a window onto your lap. It feels good. You watch Haven go through his ritual. There's something strange about him, you think. Haven looks up from his papers and flashes you a nervous grin, then goes back to his sorting. You close your eyes, lean back, and relax.

The next thing you know, Matt is gently shaking you awake. "Time to go. The plane is coming in."

Turn to page 7.

"All right. The truck it is, Matt," you say.

"Then let's go!"

You give one last look at Bill, the pilot. You'd like to take him along—he's been a good friend—but it's more important that Mimla, Matt, Haven, and you get away.

You grab your kit and start to leave the Windmaster, but suddenly you have a thought. Quickly you raid the plane's lockers, throwing everything that might be useful out the door: first-aid kit, blankets, rope, food, and last, the submachine gun stashed under the pilot's seat. You jump out of the plane. Matt drives the truck to the Windmaster's side and rapidly stows the supplies.

It seems to take forever, but in two minutes you're all loaded into the truck, a 2005 Chevy Blazer four-wheel drive—old, but serviceable. You head north, toward Turtalia.

Turn to page 19.

When the plane is stable, you feel an incredible rush of relief. Matt instantly notices your pale and queasy appearance.

"Hey, relax," he says. "You did it! I'll take the controls for a while. I can handle it, and you could use a little rest."

Gratefully you remove your hands from the control stick. You'll be all right in a minute or two.

"Those were Doradan troops out there," Matt says as you slump back in your seat. "I saw them as we climbed out. It's a good thing we left."

Turn to page 18.

18

"Sure is," you say, straightening up a bit. You feel much better already. "I wonder what we should do now."

"What do you mean? I thought we were flying out of here."

"We are, but maybe we should circle for a while first. I'm also not sure if we should head directly for Denver. The clouds around us remind me how violent the weather can be in the mountains."

You are sitting up straight now. Talking has helped you a lot. "Flying in these mountains in bad weather is no picnic," you add.

"I get your point," Matt says. "But we've got a lot to lose. We really have to try to get Bill to a doctor. I think we should head to Denver now."

If you decide to follow Matt's instincts and fly straight to Denver, turn to page 24.

If you decide to follow your instincts and circle while you examine the possibilities, turn to page 22.

"Better get off the road," Matt suggests. "Keep to the scrub—there'll be less dust that way. Maybe they'll be so busy with the plane they won't notice us."

Soon you're out of sight of the barn and the forlorn-looking Windmaster. The column of dust from the Doradan troops, if that's who it really is, is much closer. You certainly couldn't stick around to find out.

"I took a good look before we disappeared over that rise," Matt says. "I think they'll be at the plane in about ten minutes."

Matt is interrupted by a low BA-DOOM!!

You shudder. "Bazooka-launched rocket," you say. "It must be the Doradan Secret Police."

Turn to page 38.

"Mimla's right," you say. "Our chances are much better if we separate. She and I will head for Santa Fe. I know of a 'safe house' there. We can meet in two days. OK, Matt?"

"I don't like it. I'm responsible for Mimla, and the four of us would be better off staying together if there's a fight."

But Mimla is firm, and so are you. Matt finally agrees. Haven remains quiet; he looks scared.

"Here, Matt. This is the location of the safe house." You show him a map of downtown Santa Fe. The safe house is just two blocks west of the main plaza.

You all shake hands and prepare to leave.

At that very moment there is a knock at the door—a loud knock! Mimla raises a finger to her lips. Haven cringes in the corner as if he's trying to imitate a piece of furniture. Everyone looks at you.

If you tell them to run for it through the back door of the house, turn to page 40.

If you tell them to prepare to defend yourselves, turn to page 29.

"You're right, Matt," you say. "If the four of us split up, our chances are no better. We need the protection of the group. It's just good sense to have more eyes and ears."

Matt is already busy with a map, plotting an escape route through the Sangre de Cristo Mountains to Denver.

"It's going to be a long haul," he says.

"Well, at least there's that safe house in Santa Fe that I was told about," you say. "We can stop there before we go into the mountains."

You and Mimla pore over the map along with Matt. Haven sits quietly, absorbed in thoughts he shares with no one.

Mimla suggests avoiding the mountains by going east. "We can get to Denver by the flatland route," she says.

"Mim, that's really dangerous!" you exclaim. "Out there, with only the sagebrush for cover, we'd be sitting ducks from the air."

She nods. "That's exactly it. The Doradans will expect us to head into the mountains. They'd never think we'd make for the flats. But let's not argue. Let's decide and get going."

If you decide to take the mountain route, with the first stop in Santa Fe, turn to page 33.

If you decide to take the flatland route, turn to page 42.

"Matt, I want to circle here a bit. Let's get used to the plane and watch the weather for a while."

"OK," he agrees. "But just for a little while."

The plane feels good in your hands. It responds well to your commands, and soon you almost forget you're not really a pilot. You're concerned about the weather, though.

"Matt, I don't like the looks of this," you say.

"How so?"

"The clouds keep building, getting more and more nasty. We won't be able to see once we're inside them. That means we'll have to fly by instruments. Plus, it looks as if they have violent winds in them. That could be really bad. And then there's the chance of hail and the plane icing up . . ."

"You make it sound impossible!" says Matt. "It's not impossible. Just not good. Besides, what other choice do we have?"

"We could go back."

"No way," you hear Mimla shout.

"I agree," Matt, says. "It could be death for Mimla. It could be death for us all."

Go on to the next page.

Then you have a thought. "I wonder if we can get a weather forecast from Dorado."

"But doing that means breaking radio silence," Matt says. "They could home in on us and blow us out of the sky."

Haven looks uneasy at this prospect, and you're not too happy about it either.

"Still," you say, "it'd give us some information. I think I can make up a fake message that won't give us away."

If you decide to break radio silence and try to get a weather forecast, turn to page 35.

If you decide to maintain silence and see if you can come up with another idea, turn to page 39.

"Time is too precious to waste it flying in circles," you say. "We've got to get the Doradan invasion plans to Turtalia!"

But first you have to get over the mountains and on to Denver. There is no other way for you, and Mimla strongly agrees with Matt. She wants to continue the fight against Doradan brutality at any risk.

The cumulus clouds tower about you, and the plane is bouncing around in the turbulence. You crane your neck, scanning the sky for some break in the clouds below.

It's a tough decision. Should you descend through the clouds in search of clearer airspace and face the danger of crashing into a mountain peak? Or should you climb higher to get over the clouds and face the danger of running into even more turbulence?

If you descend, turn to page 37.

If you climb, turn to page 30.

The plane noses into a dive again, then starts spinning wildly. The spin throws Haven off balance. He goes crashing to one side of the cockpit, dazed. You grab for the controls.

The Windmaster levels off. Matt comes running forward with the rope. Mimla is close behind him.

"What happened?" Matt yells.

"Tie him up. Quickly." You're busy trying to gain altitude.

Just as Matt gets near him, Haven screams and flails his arms. Matt and Mimla can't get close enough to subdue him. Haven seems berserk; he hits the control panel wildly, knocking at switches and dials.

"Stop him!" you shout.

Too late! Haven has hit the transmit switch on the transponder. The plane is now broadcasting a signal that reports its location. Doradan pursuit planes are probably homing in on you already.

Turn to page 27.

Matt throws a punch and Haven goes down. Matt and Mimla truss him up like a chicken in a matter of seconds.

"He'll be no more trouble now," Mimla says.

You reach for the transponder to turn it off. Instead, you pull your hand away again.

"What?" Mimla asks.

"The Doradans will find it very strange if our transponder suddenly goes off the air," you answer.

"But what choice do we have?" she says.

"My father taught me some Doradan codes. I can try to fake it by inventing a false ID and a secret mission." You look outside. "Or, I can turn off the transponder and try to hide in the clouds."

If you flick off the transponder and head for the clouds, turn to page 105.

If you try to fake it, pick up the mike and turn to page 53.

Taos it is. "It's near the Turtalian-Doradan border," you explain to Matt. "We need to get out of this turbulence."

You do a rough calculation based on your last known position, your airspeed, the wind speed and direction, and your own gut feeling of where you are.

"I figure we're probably right over Taos at this very moment," you announce.

According to the last reports, the Taos regime has remained independent. Taos is free of Doradan control except for an occasional military patrol to prevent the Pueblos from becoming actively hostile to the Doradans. Mimla will be safe there.

You feel good about this decision. As you slip through the clouds, the outline of mountains and valley and desert floor appears below you.

The landing is tricky but possible. Deep in your memory is all the flight instruction you had from your father: "Set up your approach. Don't drop your airspeed too rapidly or you'll stall. Don't be low and slow. Flare at the right time to spill air, and create a planned stall just as you touch down."

Turn to page 68.

You nod toward the pile of weapons Julio has hidden in his house. Matt and Mimla grab them and start to load. They're old M-16s left over from the territorial wars and colonial conflicts of the 2020s and '30s. Mimla tosses one to you.

Once again the knock reverberates through the house. Then you hear a faint voice.

"*Amigos. Mis amigos*, do not be afraid. It is me, Julio. Open—open, please."

You glance at your watch. It is almost five o'clock, a dangerous hour: for the last three years, the Doradan rulers have set a five o'clock curfew. Anyone seen on the street between five PM and six AM can be shot on sight. Doradan troopers of the Elite Squad patrol the city. To them, shooting people out on the streets is a game.

"Julio, use the code-knock, please," you say. You haven't heard the prearranged knock yet: three short, one long, and two short.

Julio's only response is, "*Amigos*, let me in, please."

Your watch reads 4:58.

If you open the door, turn to page 59.

If you insist on the special knock, turn to page 117.

It looks rough above, but you'd rather face turbulence than the terror of hitting some cloud-covered mountain peak.

The Windmaster responds nicely to your control movements, making a spiraling climb through the vapor-laden whiteness. For several moments you enjoy the sheer pleasure of flying, remembering calmer days when your dad sat behind you in a sleek orange Swiss-built sailplane, teaching you the freedom of flight.

Suddenly you top out above the clouds in bright sunlight that immediately warms the cabin.

"Not bad! Boy, I hope the whole flight is like this," Matt exclaims.

"Well, let's just hope that we can get back down through these clouds when we reach Denver. That's when Bill would have been the most help."

Mimla has been quiet, but she suddenly speaks.

"Look! Look!"

She points to the two o'clock position. You see three patrol planes out the window. Sunlight glints off the bright green and blue markings of Dorado emblazoned on their wings.

Turn to page 49.

You pick up the microphone. "Calling any Turtalian base. Repeat, any Turtalian base. We are in trouble. Need help in landing our plane. The pilot is unconscious, perhaps dead. Repeat, SOS. Anybody out there?"

For several tense moments you strain your ears, waiting for a response. Then it comes.

"Turtalian advance base to aircraft in trouble. Head out on a course of forty degrees northeast, altitude fourteen thousand feet. Air speed of one hundred knots. We will pick you up and guide you home."

Matt slaps you on the back. "Sounds good. We'll make it!"

Then the radio comes to life again.

"Windmaster in trouble. We read you. This is a Turtalian base. We will send escort craft to pick you up and guide you in. Maintain present altitude, circle, and leave your transponder on. Help is on the way."

"Well, there we are," Matt says. "Two answers. Which one is real? One of them has to be the Doradans."

*If you follow the first set of instructions,
turn to page 71.*

If you follow the second set, turn to page 87.

"We have to go the mountain route," you say. "There are friendly guerrilla groups and partisans in the hills."

Mimla nods in agreement with your logic. Now it's up to you to lead the escape.

"We haven't got much time," you say. "The region will be crawling with patrols now that they've downed our escape plane. They'll search the area around the airstrip and go north from there. We'll actually be behind them—unless, that is, they figure out that we've come back into town."

You keep an eye on the Secret Police building across the street. There is a lot of activity: jeeps, jitneys, and an occasional staff car coming and going. Then you see them: two men in their early sixties. One is grotesquely fat, with triple chins and bulging eyes. Diamond rings punctuate his stubby fingers.

The other man is trim and short, dressed in a well-tailored uniform without insignia of any kind. You recognize him. He's the head of the Doradan Secret Police, and he's walking across the street toward your hideout!

Turn to page 46.

"I've got a way to break radio silence and not be recognized," you say.

As you pick up the mike to radio for a weather forecast, Haven becomes hysterical.

"We're all going to die!" he shrieks. He repeats it, calmly this time, almost in a monotone: "We're-all-going-to-die."

Then he lunges for the controls.

The Windmaster starts to dive as you fend him off. Matt and Mimla grab Haven and pull him away. He shakes them off and crouches in a corner of the cabin, near Bill's unconscious form. Haven is breathing rapidly; his eyes are glazed. You pull the plane out of its dive just in time.

"What do we do now?" Matt asks in a low voice, jerking his head toward Haven.

You give Haven a quick glance.

He looks better. His breathing is quieter and less labored. Some color is coming back into his cheeks. But you suspect he could blow again at any moment.

"Tie him up," you murmur to Matt. Matt goes off to get some rope. Without warning, Haven jumps for the controls again. You try to knock him back, but his craziness seems to give him superhuman strength. He's winning!

Turn to page 25.

"The landing strip at Taos is too risky," you argue.

After you explain your reasons, Matt finally agrees that you should avoid it. You still haven't solved your problems, though: the turbulence in the clouds you're flying through could rip a wing off the Windmaster.

"Hey, Matt," you say. "What's your guess on how far it is to the West Coast?"

Matt pores over the charts. Haven peers up from his doodling. He looks anxious, as usual. "California is not safe. I know it's not a safe place."

You and Matt exchange glances. "I don't agree," Matt says. "California isn't controlled by any group. We stand as good a chance of making it there as anywhere."

You nod agreement. But Mimla does not. She grips Matt by the arm and says, "I have reason to believe that Haven is right. California isn't safe. Let's put the plane down in Taos."

Matt looks uncomfortable. After all, he was entrusted to accompany Mimla and help her escape to Turtalia.

Turn to page 70.

You're not sure you can handle the motor-glider in turbulence. You push the control column forward, sending the Windmaster into a steep dive through the clouds. You kick the rudder pedals hard and sideslip down to 13,000 feet before leveling off.

You're in luck. The cloud cover ends abruptly, and at last you have enough visibility and room to fly. Mountains surround you. You weave around them. The air currents are tricky, and the rock faces and tree-covered slopes seem too close for comfort.

"Any suggestions, Matt?" you ask. "I haven't the faintest idea where we are."

Matt shakes his head. "No, we're up against it. We could radio to the Turtalians for help."

"Yes, but that's dangerous. The Doradans could beam in on us, and then it'd be all over."

If you radio for Turtalian help, turn to page 32.

If you continue on, using your intuition,
turn to page 54.

The sound of the explosion finally stops echoing in the hills. "Well, they must have gotten the plane as soon as they could see it," Matt says after a pause.

"I wonder if they've seen us?" you ask nobody in particular.

"No way of telling," Matt answers. He glances around the truck. Mimla looks alert and ready to do whatever is necessary. Haven looks so pale that he might pass out at any time.

"We have to decide what to do," you say.

"And with no information," Mimla adds. "I wish we knew if they'd spotted us, or assumed we were in the plane, or if they've called in search planes, or . . ."

"Hold on," you say. "It doesn't make any difference. We have to get out of here, no matter what. We have two ways to travel now: in the Blazer or on foot. The Blazer is faster, but it's easier for them to spot. Walking is slower, but it's easier for us to hide." You bang the steering wheel with your hands. "I wish I knew which one to choose. "

"Got a coin?" Matt asks with a smile.

"No," you say, "I'll make the decision myself."

If you decide to abandon the Blazer and head out on foot, turn to page 41.

If you decide to keep going in the Blazer, turn to page 50.

"A fake radio message is just the sort of slipup the Secret Police are waiting for," you tell Matt. "We'll keep radio silence."

This is dangerous, because you really need as much help as you can get with this plane. The air has gotten bumpy and flying takes all your concentration.

Matt finds a map case with a sectional flight map of the region you're in.

"Look at this!" he cries. "There's an emergency strip just a little north of Taos. Let's head for it."

You take a quick glance, just enough to see that the strip is nestled in the region close to Kachina Peak. It could be tough making that approach in clouds. One big mistake and WHAMMO!

If you decide to land at the abandoned strip in Taos, turn to page 28.

If you decide to keep on flying in the general direction of Denver, turn to page 36.

40

"We have to get out of here," you whisper. "Come on, Mimla, out the back way."

All four of you dash for the back door. You get to it first and open it. You stick your head out, then whisper, "All clear. Come on."

The door leads out to a back alley that winds through a maze of streets behind stores, office buildings, and a few large apartment buildings.

As you enter the alley you realize Haven isn't with you.

"Hey, where's Haven?" You look around. Mimla and Matt shake their heads.

"We can't leave him," you say.

Matt looks disgusted. "Don't bother looking for him. We can't waste time. He'll have to fend for himself. Let's go."

But you stay. Haven is a member of your team. Should you endanger the whole mission by going back for him, or leave him to take care of himself?

If you go back to look for Haven, turn to page 102.

If you go on and leave Haven behind, turn to page 60.

"Let's get going on foot," you say. "It's slower, but safer."

You turn the Blazer down a gully and park it under an overhang. It's well-hidden there.

Quickly the four of you unload everything useful from the truck and make manageable bundles out of it. Matt grabs the submachine gun. "I'm a first-class marksman," he says, without bragging.

"Let's hope it won't come to that," you reply.

You finish tucking your gear into your makeshift pack and stand up. Matt is almost done with his, and you turn to check how Mimla and Haven are doing.

Mimla is nearly finished as well, but you don't see Haven.

You turn in a circle, scanning the area. "Matt, where's Haven?"

Matt lifts his head. "Dunno. He was here a minute ago. Maybe he's in the bushes."

The three of you search for several minutes, but you don't find Haven.

Turn to page 48.

"All right, Mimla," you agree. "Let's take the flatland route."

She peers out the window. "Good. Albuquerque's curfew has begun, though. We can't start until morning."

The night passes very slowly, punctuated by the occasional sounds of gunfire. Finally dawn spreads across the eastern sky.

The curfew ends at six AM. Disguised as Doradan militia on your way to weekly training, you prepare to leave. In Dorado, all citizens must serve in the militia, although only the regular military have weapons. The day of your training is assigned by lottery. ID cards are

issued to all Doradans, complete with physical description, date of birth, and a number, from one to seven, indicating your training day.

Julio has a stock of militia uniforms. He has been busy most of the night preparing your ID cards, all with the number 4 in the upper right corner. It is not easy work. The Doradans will shoot first and ask questions later if they suspect the cards are phony.

"All set?" Matt asks. "We'll go singly to the square and then regroup and take a jitney as though we were heading for a training site. Once we're in the flatlands, we'll look for our chance to escape."

Turn to page 58.

"Search Haven," you order Matt.

Haven is not strong enough to stop him. Matt searches his clothing and finds a Doradan Secret Police ID card hidden in the lining of his jacket.

At six PM sharp there is a tap on the back door. You open it.

"There is no time to delay," the head of the Secret Police says. He motions you to a government limousine waiting nearby in the alley.

You all pile in. Haven, tied and gagged, is put in the trunk. The driver zooms off into the night to a fuel supply depot on the outskirts of town. There Haven is taken away by two men in blue coveralls.

You, Mimla, and Matt are hidden in a special section of a sixteen-wheel oil tanker. Its engines rumble, and soon you're on your way to Santa Fe, the mountains, and finally Denver.

The adventure is over, for now. But with Mimla free and the plans for the Doradan invasion in your hands, the future looks bright for Turtalia.

The End

You're so frightened that you can't even speak. You motion to the others to be quiet. The fat man gets into a car and roars off, leaving a cloud of fumes behind.

The other man walks directly to the door of Julio's house, where you're hiding. You watch him through a sliver of an opening behind some window curtains. He stops, pulls out a pack of gum, removes a stick, and

Go on to the next page.

drops the pack in front of the door. He examines the door as if looking at an art work in a museum, then stoops to tie his shoelace—which is already tied. He speaks in a voice that's almost a whisper.

"Read the message in the pack of gum. NAMASTE!"

You almost collapse from fear and surprise. Namaste is the Turtalian code word given to you by your father to identify agents. No one knows it but you and top-secret Turtalian agents in Dorado.

Can you trust the head of the secret police? Is he really an agent of Turtalia—or did he get the code word Namaste by torturing one of your people?

If you open the door to read the message in the pack of gum, turn to page 65.

If you think you better escape out the back door instead, turn to page 40.

"Haven must have run away," Matt says.

"But why?" you and Mimla ask together.

"Scared, maybe? People do funny things when they're frightened."

"Well, what do we do now? We need those computer codes he's got. Do we look for him or leave him?"

Mimla's question hangs in the dry desert air.

If you decide to abandon Haven,
turn to page 84.

If you search for Haven, turn to page 116.

SECRET ONLINE ENDING

If you decide Haven is a traitor and risk a broadcast to the Turtalian radio system warning of his departure, go to
www.cyoa.com/escape94212.htm

"Wow! Where did they come from? How did they know we were here?" you exclaim.

Matt scans the sky with binoculars. "Those are prop planes."

"They're not very fast, but fast enough. What do you think, Matt and Mimla?" you ask. "Have they seen us?"

"Not yet, but they will at any moment," Matt answers. "What are our chances if we try to outrun them?"

You estimate that your distance from the patrol planes is a little over six miles. You are hovering right above the cloud cover. The wind is with you, and with engines at full-throttle, you could reach an airspeed of 150 knots.

If you make a run for it, you could cross into Turtalian airspace, but the patrol planes will probably follow anyway. If you duck back into the clouds, they will just circle around until you come out again.

If you try to outrun the patrol planes, turn to page 57.

If you duck back into the clouds, turn to page 52.

50

"Look, if we stay with the Blazer we can get farther away," you say. "They probably won't spot us before we spot them. If they do, we can leave the truck then."

"Good thinking," Mimla says. "Matt, check out those maps in the glove compartment, and find the best route. Haven, keep an eye out for the Doradans." Then she has a second thought. "I'll keep a lookout, too."

You concentrate on driving. It's tough work. You have to detour around the large trees and the cacti while still keeping your speed up. At the same time, you're looking in the rearview mirror, watching the dust cloud the truck kicks up and trying to keep it as small as possible. The dust cloud could draw the attention of the Doradan Secret Police—unless they spot the truck from the air.

Matt keeps looking up from the maps spread on his knees to check his bearings and the lay of the land.

"We're pretty exposed where we are," he says. "There's not much in the way of hiding places. To the northwest the terrain gets a little better, but it's not the direction we want to go. The way we want to go is blocked by the Continental Divide."

"What about going over the divide?" you ask.

"There's only one pass close by. How's this for a name: 'Satan Pass'?"

Go on to the next page.

"Satan Pass. Sounds grisly," you say.

"The road's probably in grisly shape, too," Matt says. "We could also stay west of the divide and drive parallel to it. The only trouble is, we'd be exposed on the road."

"Is that Highway 56?" You've been sneaking glances at the maps.

"Yes."

"Wait a minute," Mimla says. "So far we have no reason to think that the Secret Police know we're here or that we're driving a Blazer. If we take the highway we'll just look like an ordinary truck. And we can have three pairs of eyes on the lookout."

"Not a bad idea, Mimla," you respond. "But there's good cover up in Satan Pass; we'd be hard to spot. It also doesn't seem like the direction that we'd choose to go—if the police are looking for us, they probably won't check it out."

*If you decide to head over Satan Pass,
turn to page 86.*

*If you decide to stay west of the divide and try
Highway 56, turn to page 91.*

52

"Back into the clouds," you decide aloud. "No way can we outrun those planes."

The Windmaster bumps several times in the turbulence. Then you're enveloped by the white cloud vapor.

The radio comes to life.

"This is Turtalian Free Land radio base. We have you on our radar. Identify yourself with proper code."

Safety! But only if you use the proper codes. You find the identification codes in a small canvas pouch along with the flight maps and charts. They are to be used only in emergencies. Surely this is one.

Turn to page 96.

You pick up the microphone and begin broadcasting to the Doradans.

"Gallup Base. This is mission Y-niner. We are initiating phase number three. Over."

Matt looks questioningly at you. You'd like to plan what you're doing, but you can't take the time right now. You are thinking furiously while you wait for a Doradan response to your transmission. You wave Matt to be quiet.

"Y-niner. This is Gallup Base. Who the devil are you? Over."

"Gallup Base. Code One, please. Repeat, Code One. Authorization zebra-delta-baker-five. Over."

A light film of sweat covers your forehead. If your father's code information is correct, you have told Gallup Base you are in the middle of a secret reconnaissance mission with the highest of Doradan security priorities. Right now there should be a mad scramble at Gallup Base while codes are being checked and—

The radio crackles. "Y-niner. Please stand by. Over."

Uh-oh, you think. Either you've blown the code or the Doradans are so disorganized that they need time to figure it out.

Turn to page 62.

"Using the radio is too risky," you say to Matt. "We're going to have to navigate by instinct."

Once again you enter the cloud cover. You circle briefly until you spot another opening, then descend into clear space. Once again luck is with you: the area is relatively open.

"Look! Look to the left," cries Mimla. "See? Down there! It looks like a landing strip."

"I think you're right, Mimla," you say. "Good eyes. Let's try it."

Your heart thumping and your hands clammy on the wheel, you descend toward the isolated emergency landing strip.

Turn to page 74.

"We'll run for it," you say. "Those three planes will never get us."

You hope you're right. You open the throttles wide and head for Denver.

Suddenly, right ahead of you, there is one more plane bearing the green and blue Doradan squares. Your Windmaster is wreathed in a halo of tracer bullets.

Your last thought is, "Why can't the world be peaceful?"

The End

Clutching your phony ID cards, the four of you line up at Julio's back door. You leave at four minute intervals.

You wish your companions good luck. Matt walks out first—strong, tough-looking, confident. He scowls a little to complete the picture of a loyal Doradan militiaman who hopes to make it into the full-time military—a highly paid elite with special privileges and rights.

Next is Mimla, who has been waiting calmly. She too walks out confidently, turns the corner at the end of the alley, and disappears. Now it's Haven's turn. He hesitates, fidgeting with the sand-colored gun belt around his waist.

"I can't do it," he wails. "They'll catch me. I can't do it!"

You grab him by the arm and push him through the door.

"Yes, you can. I'm with you."

You practically have to drag him down the dark alley toward the square, which puts you right in front of Doradan Secret Police headquarters. You don't like this one bit. Haven is trembling, ashen-faced, and unsteady on his feet. He could break at any moment. Just one look from a tough Doradan and it might be all over.

Turn to page 98.

"Cover me, Matt," you say. "I'll open the door on three."

You edge up to the door and count in a voice just loud enough for the others in the room to hear you:

"One . . . two . . ."

On three you shove the heavy wooden door forward. It groans on its iron hinges. A bolt of late afternoon sun pierces the semi-gloom of the room. Julio slips in and slams the door behind him. He leans against the door, gasping.

"Sorry, but I didn't have much time. Those monkeys in the uniforms shoot poorly, but with my luck, who knows?"

"OK, OK, Julio. What news have you brought us?" you ask.

Julio twists his hat in his hands, a somber expression on his face. You know before he speaks that the news is bad.

"*Señorita* Mimla, it is with the greatest sadness that I must inform you of the capture of your two cousins."

Julio nods in the direction of the secret police headquarters across the street. Mimla shudders. Matt goes to her and grips her hand.

"Those men were our best, our very best," Mimla gasps. "How did they get them? There must be an informer. First they caught Matt and me, now my cousins!"

Turn to page 82.

In this high-stakes game, it's each for himself. You can't go back to look for Haven. You're carrying the plans for the Doradan invasion; Mimla's the head of the resistance. All of that can't be put at risk for one person.

You give a last look back at the open doorway. Then you, Matt, and Mimla dash down the alley and make for the first open door in the seventeen-story apartment building opposite. You find yourselves in a parking garage. Matt locks the door behind you.

The cement floor is dry and gritty under your shoes. You feel as if the whole world can hear every step you take.

There are about twenty cars in the garage. The parking attendant is an old man dozing in a cubicle. His TV set is on, tuned to the only station, Doradan government TV. The sound covers your approach. You have no trouble overcoming him and tying him up. He smiles weakly at you and flashes the victory sign as you grab a set of keys from a rack over his head.

Minutes later you, Mimla, and Matt are in a two-door, silver-colored Japanese sedan. It's an old car but still in good shape.

You pull out of the garage and head north toward Santa Fe and freedom.

"We'll be home tonight," you say, and you know you're right.

The End

"Gallup Base, this is Y-niner. We copy and are changing course to one-one-seven."

You kick the rudder pedals and bring the control column over to the right. The numbers on the compass flash by: 80-90-100-110. You start to level off and steady in on your new course of 117 degrees.

"I don't like this," Matt says. "I feel uneasy. Can we do anything else?"

"Not now," you sigh as you point to the Doradan chase planes flanking you.

The fighter planes escort you to a small Doradan military airfield.

Once or twice en route you think you spy a good escape route, but you don't try it. The fighter planes carry heat-seeking missiles that are capable of blowing you to bits.

When you land, Bill is taken away in an ambulance. You are arrested and taken away for trial—in a year or two—as escapees from glorious "totalitarian freedom."

The End

It seems to be taking the Doradans forever to respond.

"Did you know you're flying with your fingers crossed?" Matt asks.

"Yes, and I'm keeping them that way." You fill Matt in on what you're doing.

"I hope it works. What do we do if it doesn't?"

"I don't know," you answer. "I don't honestly know."

The radio crackles again. "Y-niner. This is Gallup Base. Change heading to one-one-seven. Repeat, one-one-seven. Authorization override baker-five. Do you copy?"

"What does that mean?" Matt asks.

"Not sure. They want us to change our course, but the code and authorization I gave them for our mission should have had such priority that they couldn't do that."

"What's 'authorization override baker-five'?"

"That's what worries me. I've never heard of it. It leaves two possibilities. One, it's a real code and Turtalian intelligence doesn't know about it. Two, it's as fake as our ID and they know it but hope we don't."

"What do we do?" says Matt.

"Good question. Either we change heading the way they told us to and keep on faking it—or we run for it. There are no chase planes in sight. We might make it."

The radio crackles impatiently. "Y-niner. Do you copy course change?"

If you change your heading, turn to page 61.

If you run for it, turn to page 66.

"There's something suspicious about the unguarded jeep," you say. "We better go by foot."

The four of you set off on foot into the flatlands. The sun climbs high into the sky and the land shimmers with heat.

Many long days—and weeks—of hard walking lie ahead. To avoid heatstroke and dehydration, you will have to travel at night. You can only hope that you'll find enough water to keep you going.

Good luck!

The End

"It's worth a try. I'm going to open the door," you say.

Haven leaps across the room and blocks your path.

"No, no! Don't! It's a trick. A trick! We'll all be killed!"

You look at Haven, then Mimla, and finally at Matt. Haven grabs your arm. His hands are shaking.

"Please," Haven begs. "I'll find a way out for us. I swear, I'll find a way out."

Haven's words surprise everyone. He's always been so quiet.

"Step aside," you say. "I've made my decision."

He lets go of your arm and draws himself up. "You'll have to go through me," he says, suddenly defiant.

Outside the light is growing dimmer. Soon it will be time for curfew.

*If you decide to push Haven aside,
turn to page 103.*

*If you decide Haven must have a good reason to
prevent you from opening the door,
turn to page 76.*

Run for it! It seems like the best thing to do. You flick off the transponder but leave the radio on.

The sky is filled with clouds, and there is an especially large one near your plane. The radio crackles on.

"Y-niner. Come in, Y-niner. This is Gallup Base. Code nine. Code nine. Come in, Y-niner. This is Gallup Base. Sir, they're not . . ." The radio cuts out. You're surrounded by silence and the white cloud.

"There should be planes here any minute. Let's hope they don't find us."

Then you have an idea! you have been watching the variometer since you entered the cloud. The instrument has shown large masses of steadily rising air. Quickly you start flying the Windmaster in a tight circle and turn the engines off.

"What? Are you crazy?" Matt yells.

"Hang on. Calm down. This plane has a glide ratio of twenty to one. I don't know if we can climb, but we should be able to maintain our altitude. The wind will cool off the exhausts in a few minutes. They won't find us unless they blunder right into us."

"I hope you're right," Matt says in a doubtful tone.

"Me, too."

You are right. The Windmaster holds her altitude, perhaps even climbs a few feet every turn. With your eye on the instruments, you start flipping the radio through the broadcast bands.

"Search Leader to base, negative sighting," a voice says.

Go on to the next page.

"That's them!" you whisper to Matt. You're not sure why you're whispering. They couldn't hear you even if you opened a window and shouted at the top of your lungs.

"Base to Search Leader, continue search," a second voice says.

"Search Leader to Search One, check that cloud."

You turn to Matt and hold up one hand; your fingers are crossed. Matt holds up both his hands with a grin; all his fingers are crossed.

A couple of minutes pass, then: "Search One to Search Leader, negative. Wait! I've got them sighted, just below me!"

You gulp hard and frantically search the sky. The cloud has thinned out a bit above you, and you catch a glimpse of a Doradan fighter. Then the cloud thickens again.

"Search Leader to Search One. Climb hard. Missile away. Fire!"

Turn to page 113.

You wish this was just another practice landing with your dad. But this one is all yours, and it's for real.

As quickly as the clouds break up, they come back. You start to panic as you approach the airstrip.

Hold on. Bank. Kick the starboard pedal. Push the stick slightly forward and move it to the starboard. Ease in more power. Watch the altimeter! Careful! Careful!

The clouds break. You are just south of the strip, about 1,000 feet above it. You go into the final approach, release flaps, and keep your airspeed near 100 knots.

Touchdown! The rubber tires squeak, then roll on the bumpy surface.

Matt releases a long breath of relief and slaps you on the back. "Perfect landing!"

The Pueblo Indians in the area welcome you. They give you shelter and food and take care of Bill, the sick pilot. In the spring, when the snow pack melts, you will cross the mountain passes on your way to Denver.

Well done. Congratulations!

The End

"We've already decided Taos is too dangerous," you say to Mimla.

She slumps back in her seat. After all, you're the pilot and in command. This time your decision remains firm, and the Windmaster heads west.

You have enough gas to get to the Los Angeles area. The weather improves after just forty minutes of flying away from Taos. "Not bad!" you say. "We'll make it OK."

You sound cheerful and encouraging, but no one else in the plane is smiling. Mimla looks furious, Haven keeps doodling, and Matt stares out at the horizon.

"Turn up the radio, will you, Matt? We're getting something."

Matt fiddles with the tuning and volume dials. There's the usual snap and pop. Then the signal becomes clear—too clear. It's a string of battle commands from ground troops and helicopter strike-forces. There seem to be well-armed gangs, probably former soldiers, operating across the entire Los Angeles area.

You'll reach the L.A. zone in less than an hour. Maybe it's the wrong place to land. Perhaps you should head north toward what's left of San Francisco. It has supposedly been devastated by fire and bombing, but it might still be safer.

If you go on toward Los Angeles, turn to page 106.

If you head north toward San Francisco, turn to page 108.

"I'm going with the first set of instructions," you say to Matt. "They gave a 40-degree NE compass heading, which is about right for the Denver area. Besides that, the second set identified us as a Windmaster. Only the Doradans are searching for our Windmaster; the Turtalians at central command are keeping the mission a secret. A Turtalian base receiving our message wouldn't know what aircraft we're in."

"Brilliant," Matt agrees.

You swing out on the 40-degree NE heading, climb to 14,000 feet, and head homeward. Constant guidance from the Turtalian base brings you safely over the mountains. Occasionally you see the peaks of the Rockies poking up through the gauzy clouds.

Once you are over the mountains, you are directed to begin a shallow descent to the airfield at Denver. The cloud cover is deep and you enter a silent world of whiteness. It seems like a long dream as you slip through the clouds.

Turn to page 79.

"I'm not leaving," you say firmly. "First of all, someone has to take care of Bill. Second, it's nonsense to leave. We have a better chance to be found here than if we go wandering around like jackrabbits in the wilderness. You go if you want."

Mimla sneers at you. Matt shrugs his shoulders and says, "Well, I'm with her—even though you're probably right. Good luck. Godspeed."

Haven joins Mimla and Matt. The three of them start off, and soon they're lost to sight.

You build a fire from dried pinon branches. The smoke smells good. At the end of the second day, Bill suddenly trembles convulsively, then lies back, quiet. He is dead.

You run out of food. The days merge into each other. Hallucinations of friends, warm sunny beaches, and sumptuous meals fill your waking hours. You drift in soft waves of warmth and cold. One afternoon you hear voices, but you're sure they're only more hallucinations.

They're not! It's a Turtalian rescue party. You are saved.

The End

The land comes up to meet you before you can think about it. The Windmaster sets down on the scrubby, short mountain airstrip, bumping violently. The landing gear on the starboard side rips off, and the plane spins in a cloud of dust and dry snow. There is a horrible ripping noise as the aft section twists like a piece of paper, jamming the door.

Then there is silence. You quickly hit the switches and cut the ignition to prevent the Windmaster from catching fire. The canopy over the cockpit is jammed, too, but Matt's adrenaline is pumping, lending him tremendous strength. He smashes the catch and forces the Plexiglas plastic bubble open. Cold wind greets you as the four of you scramble out, dragging Bill with you.

Minutes later you are all huddled in a ramshackle cabin beside the strip. It can barely keep the wind out, but at least you're on the ground and in one piece.

Mimla takes charge. "Matt, you and Haven gather brush and cover the plane. Otherwise the Doradans will spot it the minute the weather clears. Cover up the landing marks in the snow, too!"

She turns to you and says, "We've got a serious decision to make."

Turn to page 80.

"Relax, Haven, I won't open the door," you say, backing off.

He exhales a sigh of relief. "It's not quite curfew yet," he says. "We can still get out through the back door."

You all agree that it's time to leave. You split up and take off in different directions in the maze of alleys behind Julio's house.

Weeks later you—and you alone—succeed in getting to Denver with the help of resistance groups in Santa Fe and in the mountains. You deliver the Doradan invasion plans. The Turtalian forces use them to set up ambushes and soundly crush the Doradan invaders.

When Dorado has been liberated, you enter Albuquerque along with the Turtalian liberating forces. You are greeted by the thin man who was head of the Doradan Secret Police. But in reality, he was a Turtalian agent. The message in the pack of gum had said to beware of Haven, who was a double agent.

Now begins the hard, but hopeful, task of building a new democratic state in what was once Dorado and is now part of Turtalia. But for you, the grim task of finding out what happened to your friends must come first.

The End

Going straight to Denver may not be impossible, but you don't want to press your luck. "Santa Fe looks like a better bet right now," you tell the others.

You gather everything useful from the Blazer and divide it into manageable bundles. Matt covers the truck with some brush.

The road over the pass and down the other side is easy for walking. You don't think the truck would have made it much farther anyway.

Several times you have to hide in the bushes from Doradan patrols, but you eventually make it to your 'safe house' in Santa Fe.

Max, your contact in Santa Fe, is disappointed that you didn't make it to Denver, but he's happy you're not dead.

As he puts it, "Hey, you didn't make your escape. But at least you're alive to try again."

The End

You break out of the clouds at about 8,000 feet above the airstrip.

"This is ground control. We have you on visual, Windmaster. Circle once, gear down, airspeed one hundred ten knots, angle of descent about thirty degrees. Easy now. Watch it, your starboard wing is low. That's it. Ease back a bit. Keep it coming. You're doing fine, just fine. Ease back on the stick. Flare a bit more. OK, you got it. Pump the brakes. A bit more. Let her run it out. Keep it on the ground. Well done!"

A jeep scoots out onto the strip with three people in it. One of them is your dad.

"Congratulations!" he cries. "You made it. I see you have Mimla safe and sound. Hey, who is this?"

Haven makes a duck for it, but he's grabbed by two heavily-armed soldiers.

"We've heard about you, Haven," your dad says to him. "You're a spy. We'll trade you for one of ours."

You, Matt, and Mimla are taken to Turtalian head-quarters where you are debriefed about the Doradan invasion plans. Mimla can hardly wait to begin setting up a new network of freedom fighters in Dorado. For now, you are all safe and well.

The End

You know that as well as she does. You nod, waiting for her next sentence.

"The problem, of course, is that the pilot can't travel—and we must get out of here."

You look at Mimla and then at Bill, who is slumped in the corner of the dilapidated cabin, obviously in bad shape. There is no way he can walk out.

"What do you suggest, Mimla?"

She looks straight at you, her eyes level and firm.

"That we leave him here with what supplies we have and hope we can get back to him soon enough to save him."

You don't know what to say. It will probably be a death sentence for Bill. Your choice now really is between life and death.

Should you leave Bill behind? If so, turn to page 112.

Should you stay with Bill and let the others go? If so, turn to page 73.

"Haven's idea won't work," you say. "The Secret Police might be on to his friend. We'll have to make it on our own."

The night passes slowly. In the early dawn light, you slip one by one, at four-minute intervals, into the alley behind the house. Matt is dressed like an old woman. Mimla is wearing the jumpsuit of a Doradan soldier captured in an earlier raid. You keep wearing what you had on—jeans, shirt, and a light windbreaker.

Haven decides to stay behind. You can't say you're sorry. He'd only slow you down.

There's a bus stop right in front of the Doradan Secret Police headquarters. The three of you join the group of waiting people. It's hard to act normal when you could be discovered at any minute. The bus finally comes, though, and you, Mimla, and Matt take separate seats. Later you change buses. By noon, you're in Santa Fe. Friends welcome you to the "safe house." It's amazing, but you didn't encounter a single security check.

"The gods are watching over us," Mimla says.

Her words prove true. The next day you are off through the mountains to Denver. You know you'll make it. The Doradan invasion plan will be foiled!

The End

Matt tries to calm Mimla, but she continues in a despairing voice. "They seem to know our every move. There must be a spy here. It's the only explanation!"

"Who would do it, Mimla?" you ask. "The Doradans are mad. They're killers, crooks. Who would work for them?"

Mimla shakes her head. Her voice is nearly a shriek. "That's the point! They corrupt people with money and power. They buy people's souls with bribery and intimidation."

Who is the traitor?

You look at Matt. No, it just couldn't be Matt. Julio? No, he's been risking his life for years hiding resistance people. Haven, then? You look at him, ashen-faced and cowering in the corner. He wouldn't have the guts to act as a double agent. Yet, who knows?

Matt, meanwhile, has been eyeing you. After all, you are the newcomer to the group.

"At any rate, it's time to leave," you say. "Staying here is suicide. The Doradans are probably watching us this very minute."

Turn to page 104.

"It's more important that we get Mimla and the invasion plans to safety," you say. "Haven is on his own. We can live without his computer codes."

"Let's go, then," Matt says.

You take the important stuff from Haven's pack—a canteen, spare matches, some jerky—and then you set off.

You lead, Mimla follows, and Matt brings up the rear, stopping now and then to erase your footprints with a piece of brush he has cut. Steadily you walk away from the Blazer and toward freedom.

Suddenly a low-flying plane scatters you into hiding.

"Don't look up!" Mimla yells as you dart under the brush. When the sound of the plane recedes in the distance, you ask Mimla why she said that.

"A face shows up clearly from the air. Much more clearly than the outline of a person's back. Always look down when someone is searching for you from the air and you don't want to be seen."

You camp for the night in a dark canyon. The night becomes cold as the sun goes down; you're glad you have blankets. During the night you are awakened many times by the sound of planes overhead, but you're well-hidden and you sleep securely.

The next day you continue—and so do the air searches. Because of the planes, you are forced to alter your course. You're still going north, but you have to bear west rather than east—the direction you want to go.

Turn to page 124.

You don't know what to say. All of you are over-whelmed with gratitude.

Finally Matt speaks. "Thank you."

Then both Mimla and you say, "Yes, thank you."

The voice responds, "Thanks are not necessary, but you are welcome. Go to sleep now. In the morning we will be on our way. We will take you to Mesa Verde. Our brothers there will help you through the mountains to Denver."

The figure stands up. You still haven't seen his face. He speaks again.

"Good night, my friends."

"Good night," you answer.

And you do enjoy a good night of sleep, knowing that tomorrow you will be on your way back to Turtalia and freedom.

The End

86

"Taking Highway 56 seems too risky," you say.

"Satan Pass sounds safer to me," Matt agrees.

"Get thee behind me, Satan Pass!" you say as you turn the wheel of the truck and head for the mountains on your right.

So far there's been no sign of Doradan troops. You wonder if they think that the four of you were on the plane when they blew it up.

"Say, Matt," you begin.

"Hm?" Matt responds as he turns away from the window.

"We left the engines running on the Windmaster, didn't we?"

Matt thinks a minute. "Yes, I think we did. In all the confusion I didn't think to turn them off."

"Neither did I. But listen: say you're a Doradan. You're checking out a report on spies escaping by plane. You come over a rise. . . "

"And the plane is there with its props turning! You blast it to pieces before it takes off."

"Right! And, of course, everybody on board is killed before they can get away." You smile at Matt.

"That's us!" He grins back at you.

"What about the truck tire tracks at the ranch—and no truck?" you ask.

"Accomplices," Matt answers quickly, "who dropped the escapees off and then left.

Turn to page 89.

You follow the second set of radio instructions.

Only later will you realize that the instructions came not from Turtalia, but from a Doradan base. The Doradans send patrol planes to your sector. The moment you poke the nose of the Windmaster above the clouds, the Doradan planes force you back to the main base near Gallup.

It's all over. Haven grins when the plane lands. The Doradans greet him as one of their own.

"What a creep!" you say to Matt and Mimla as the three of you are handcuffed and driven away to some uncertain fate. All you know for sure is that it's not a good one.

The End

"Right," you say. "We're home free—and I don't mean Dorado's 'totalitarian freedom,' either."

"Not quite. We've got to get over those." Matt points to the mountains, now very close. "And it's still a long way to Turtalia."

"Besides, the Doradans may still be with us," Haven adds.

"What do you mean?" you ask.

"I mean, they may not have followed your line of reasoning. They may be looking for this truck." Haven sounds convinced that they are.

"Could be, Haven," Matt says.

"You and Mimla better keep your eyes open," you tell Haven. "You, too, Matt. Now that we're on the road to the pass, I don't need your navigating."

The higher up you go, the worse the road gets.

"This pass sure earns its name," says Mimla.

You grunt your agreement. The road has suddenly become a gully, and you're too busy driving around the boulders to talk.

Suddenly the Blazer gives a lurch and the steering wheel jerks out of your hand.

Turn to page 90.

"What happened?" Matt asks as the truck comes to a halt.

"I think we just broke a tie rod," you answer.

You get out to look. Kneeling down to peer under the truck, you see that you were right.

"Well, that does it for the Blazer," Matt says.

"What do we do now?" Haven squeaks nervously.

"We walk," you say.

"Where?" Mimla asks.

"We're not far from the pass—about a quarter mile," Matt says. "We go there first. Then, after . . ."

"After," you say, "we either go down the other side, heading to the safe house in Santa Fe that I was told about, and then try our escape again. Or, we stay in the mountains and keep trying."

"But it's hundreds of miles to Denver," Haven blurts out.

"Right," you reply. "But it's not impossible."

*If you head over the pass to Santa Fe,
turn to page 77.*

*If you stay in the mountains and keep trying to
escape, turn to page 119.*

"I hope you're right, Mimla," you say as you turn onto Highway 56 and head north.

You decide not to take any chances: you pull off the road and head for cover whenever an airplane approaches. Once, however, Haven fails to spot a plane coming toward his side of the truck. Matt notices it, but it's too late by then. There is nowhere to go. You're forced to stay on the road in full sight. Nothing happens, though. The plane passes high overhead, and you all breathe a sigh of relief.

Matt yells at Haven, who says nothing except, "Sorry, I was thinking of something else."

You wonder what's the matter with Haven. You know he's not stupid. He's scared—it's easy to see—but that should make him more alert, not less.

Matt interrupts your thoughts. "We're getting close to Chaco Canyon. There should be some good hiding spots there. It's getting late. I think we should stop for the night, find a place to camp, and maybe stay hidden tomorrow. We can travel tomorrow night. It will be easier to hide."

"Sounds good, Matt." You're really beginning to appreciate having him along. He has a lot of sensible ideas.

Soon you come to a gravel path that turns off the road. It leads to a small hidden canyon with an over-hanging ledge large enough to hide the Blazer and all four of you under it.

Turn to the next page.

Dinner is brief and not too satisfying, but the beef jerky will keep you going.

You are lying down, trying to sleep, when you hear a twig snap nearby. You open your eyes but don't move.

Matt is lying nearby; his eyes are open, too. He winks

at you and starts to slide his hand to the submachine gun.

"I wouldn't move, if I were you," a low voice says.

Your heart stops.

Turn to page 115.

Before you have time to move, a tall figure stands in front of you.

"I am here in peace, strangers," a deep voice says.

"We are here in peace, too," you say.

The figure squats down, but you still can't see him. "Good. We have something in common. Now, please answer my questions. What are you doing on our land?"

Go on to the next page.

"Our land?" you think. You're not sure how to reply, so you say, "We're on a hunting trip. We've just camped here for the night."

"Please answer truthfully," the voice says. "Your future depends on it."

You pause. You don't know what to do. You're sure there are more people watching and listening. These could be Doradan soldiers trying to trick you, but the speaker doesn't sound like one. Still, you have to know more before you give yourselves away.

"I'd like to ask you a question," you say. "Who are you?"

The figure answers, "That is fair enough. We will trade questions, but since you are on our land, we will go first. You haven't answered my question: What are you doing on our land?"

If you decide to trust whoever this is and say, "We're escaping the Doradan Secret Police," turn to page 121.

If you decide it's too risky to trust somebody you haven't even seen, turn to page 111.

"Matt, here are the codes," you say. "Let's go for it."

"Roger," says Matt. "This is the answer to our prayers—unless it's a trap. Let's hope we don't end up at a Doradan base."

"We don't have much choice, do we?"

"No, I guess not. OK with you, Mim?"

She nods. You all forget Haven. He is like a piece of baggage—a nervous piece of baggage.

Matt keys the mike, stares at his digital watch, and speaks the code words precisely at one-second intervals.

First second: "OM."

Second second: "MANE."

He pauses for three seconds.

Sixth second: "PADME."

He pauses for two seconds.

Ninth second: "HUM."

Then he repeats the code, reversing the three second and two-second pauses. All ears in the plane are listening intently to the radio, waiting for the response from the land base below.

Sixty seconds pass.

Another thirty.

You feel fear creeping around your neck. Just suppose it was a hoax. Just suppose the anti-aircraft missiles at the land base are preparing to blow you out of the sky.

Go on to the next page.

Then the message comes across, loud and clear.

"Welcome home. Repeat, welcome home. Our identification code is MANDALA. Repeat, MANDALA. We will guide you in."

You look around the cabin. Only Haven is not grinning. "What's wrong with him, anyway?" you wonder.

The Turtalians give you landing instructions. Two of the Doradan planes try to follow you in, but Turtalian ground forces shoot them out of the sky.

Your landing is rough. The starboard wing crumples when you skid off the runway, but you're all safe.

Turtalian base command greets you. You immediately get medical attention for Bill and hand over the invasion plans. Mimla is already planning renewed activity against the Doradans, and, for now, all is well.

The End

Matt waits for you in the square in front of the Doradan Secret Police headquarters. Mimla stands at the corner on the opposite side.

"Hey, you guys, where were you? We'll be late for training." Matt shouts at you in a loud and clear voice, then talks with one of the soldiers. They both laugh at some private joke.

Mimla joins you, and the four of you gather near the jitney stand. You wish Haven would stop trembling.

Before long a dun-colored jitney arrives. Powered by solar cells, it's not too fast, but it works. Not much in this country does. The solar jitneys are left over from pre-Doradan junta days. They were manufactured in Turtalia; the only reason they are still in use is that they are simple and well-built.

Go on to the next page.

Two hours later you find yourself in the flatlands. The jitney drops you off near the training site and drives away. Though it's still early, the sun already feels hot.

"This is strange," Mimla says, surveying the area. "No one else is here."

"Look over there," Matt says. "An empty jeep."

The jeep has Doradan markings, but it's of Turtalian design. No one is guarding it.

"Not only that," you add, pointing, "there's a gas dump nearby. Those jerry cans look full."

"It's almost too good to be true," Mimla says.

"Maybe so, but this is our chance to escape," you answer. "The only question is whether to steal the jeep or go on foot."

If you decide to steal the jeep, turn to page 109.

If you decide to head away on foot, turn to page 63.

"Let's try Haven's scheme," you say. "What do we do next, Haven?"

Haven cracks a small smile, a unique gesture for him. "We must wait until dawn. I will go after midnight, when the secret police are usually off the streets, and contact my friend with the van."

Matt takes the first guard shift. You, Mimla, and Julio sleep fitfully in the living room. Outside you hear the occasional rattle of jeeps and isolated bursts of small-arms fire.

Near three AM, Matt wakes you for your shift. At six AM, the knock comes at the door. It's the one you arranged in advance: one short, two long, one short.

You open the door. There in front of you stands a squad of Doradans. The captain smiles and takes a puff on his thin cigar. "Welcome back to the secure grip of the great Doradan country!"

As you are marched across the street to the Secret Police headquarters, you catch a glimpse of Haven sitting in an unmarked car. Was he the traitor, or was he unlucky enough to be captured?

You'll probably never know.

The End

"I can't leave Haven behind," you say. "I feel responsible for him. You guys go ahead. I'm going back to look for him."

"OK, keep your shirt on. I'll come, too." Matt follows you.

Carefully you go back into the house. There is no sound. You cross the tiled kitchen floor and edge up to the living room doorway. With your back pressed to the wall, you poke your head around the doorway.

"Hands up! Don't move," says a familiar voice.

Haven stands in the room surrounded by five Doradan soldiers. He smiles and points a mean-looking laser pistol at you and Matt.

"It's all over. Our men will pick up Miss Mimla in the alley."

You gape at him. His smile grows bigger.

"Let me introduce myself," he says. "I am Haven Nightshade—captain, Doradan Secret Police."

The End

You shove Haven away from the door. He grabs your arm again. Matt pries him loose and holds him in a firm grip. You ease open the door.

The pack of gum lies crumpled in the gutter a few inches away. You reach out and grab it. The guards across the street look your way, laugh at you, and turn back to their usual routine.

Haven keeps on struggling, but Matt doesn't let go. Inside the pack of gum, in a precise hand, is written:

HAVEN DOUBLE AGENT
MEET ME BEHIND JULIO'S HOUSE
6 PM SHARP
HAVE ARRANGED ESCAPE
NAMASTE

Turn to page 44.

104

Haven steps forward.

"Mimla, I think I can get us out," he says. "I have a friend with a car. Well, it's not a car, actually, it's an old van. I can ask him to come tomorrow morning and pick us up. He even has special government passes to travel to Santa Fe and further north because he works for the health department. There's room for all of us."

Mimla glances at you, her face filled with doubt. In a land like Dorado, where terror rules, people trust only themselves. Resistance groups form, but they are broken by informers and spies.

"We have to go with Haven," Matt says. "Mimla, you're the strongest leader in Dorado: the price on your head is enormous. You have to get out before someone betrays you again. Your recapture could mean the end of any hope of resistance. The will of the people would be broken."

Mimla nods, but her face is still clouded with uncertainty. She turns to you.

If you urge her to accept Haven's offer, turn to page 100.

If you reject the offer and plan your own escape route, turn to page 81.

Hiding in the clouds seems like a good idea. You click off the transponder.

The clouds are thick, and the Windmaster slowly disappears into them. The silence in the cockpit seems ominous.

You are never seen again.

The End

No one in the plane talks. Your decision to land in Los Angeles frightens everyone, but you know there are Turtalian emissaries there. They should help you—you hope.

Minutes later, three insect-like pursuit helicopters swarm toward you on your right side. You see the grim and serious faces of the pilots and gunners. At that instant you remember that the Windmaster carries the Doradan military markings painted on by Turtalian

forces for the flight into Dorado.

The radio snaps and pops at you.

"Attack Leader, one confirmed twin-engine Windmaster bearing Doradan markings. Request permission to destroy!"

There is a moment of silence. You stare helplessly out the windshield at the helicopters. Matt is keying the mike to respond when the answer comes back from the helicopter base.

"Permission given. Destroy intruders."

It's all over for you.

The End

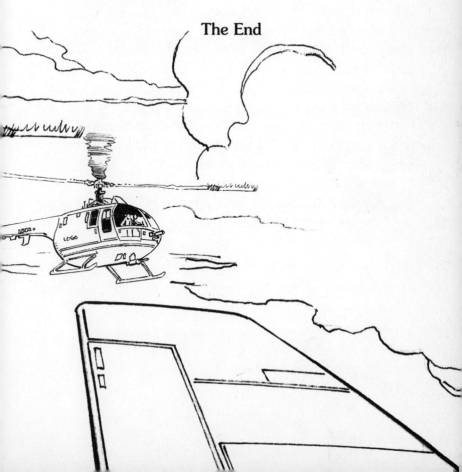

"Let's get out of here," you say. "L.A. sounds like it's a mess. The last thing we need is a combat zone. What do you think, Matt?"

"Roger. Head north."

The land below you slips by, and soon you are flying over more mountains. Straight ahead are thunderclouds. You slip between the clouds, diving and banking and climbing. It's hard to fly and monitor the compass, altimeter, and fuel all at the same time.

You begin to feel dizzy as the clouds swirl by. You lose all sense of where earth and sky are. What is up? What is down? Where are you?

Just when you are about to give up all hope, the clouds part. You see an open area below you. This is your chance!

It's rough, hilly terrain, but you do a fine job of landing. A wing tip crumples, and the landing gear is battered. Matt hits his head on the control panel and has a small cut, and Haven covers himself with vomit, but the five of you get out alive.

You are in free territory, inhabited by refugees from Los Angeles, survivors from ruined San Francisco, and hardy souls from Dorado. There is a camp about three

Stealing the jeep is easy. The keys are in the ignition. The cans at the dump are full of gas. You set off across the sagebrush flats, heading north to Denver.

Matt drives. Hours pass. Twice you're stopped by Doradan patrols, but Julio's false ID cards are good ones. Your luck holds out and you keep moving without trouble.

Two days later, after leaving the roads and going cross-country, your group enters Turtalian territory. You, along with Mimla and the Doradan invasion plans, are safe—and FREE!

The End

Your mission is too important for you to take a chance with an unseen stranger.

You try to sound casual as you say, "We're just passing through. You know, hiking, sightseeing, a little hunting."

"I wish you were telling the truth, but I can see that you are not." The voice pauses, then speaks again. "Hunters, especially three of them, don't carry only one gun—a machine gun at that. Hikers and sightseers don't sweep away their tracks."

He pauses again. You are scared. Too late, you recall the feeling you'd had that you were being watched. The voice continues.

"I will answer your question now. We are Navajos. We live here. I call it our land, but we do not believe that land can be owned. 'Our' is a word we have borrowed from white people. I think you are escaping from the scum—I cannot call them men—who rule Dorado. Do not ask for our help. We will not give it now. Some people do not lie. Those people we trust even though sometimes it brings our downfall. Those who lie, we shun."

Another figure steps out of the dark and removes the machine gun from under Matt's blankets.

"We will escort you off our land, and then we will leave you," she says. "You will not come back. You are on your own."

The End

112

It's a very difficult decision to leave Bill alone in the cabin. But you have the Doradan invasion plans and you must get out. The future of Turtalia and the lives of many people may well depend on your getting those plans back to Denver.

Outside, Matt studies the maps and points to a spot.

"I'll bet this is where we are. It doesn't matter anyway. It's all wilderness. Let's get going."

For three days you trudge in the face of wind, snow, and fatigue. You become helplessly lost in the merciless mountains. Courage and hope fade; fatigue rules your lives. Haven goes mad and runs off toward imagined safety, leaving you, Matt and Mimla.

Finally your food is gone. You grow more and more tired, but then become strangely peaceful. The incessant snowflakes seem like little friends.

At last you feel warm, contented, and happy. Mimla and Matt trudge on as you wave good-bye and slump to the ground.

The End

There is nothing you can do. The heat-seeking missile fired at you is already on its way. Its sensors reach out and detect a faint glimmer of heat. Even though you've turned off your engines and the wind has cooled the exhausts, a little heat still remains in the engines. If the missile had hands, it would rub them together now in satisfaction as it homes in on you.

Then it detects an even greater source of heat nearby. Circuits click, relays hum, and the missile instantly changes course, following the exhaust trail of Search One. Seconds later the only thing left of the missile and Search One is a rapidly expanding ball of debris.

Turn to the next page.

114

Search Leader keeps looking for you, but the cloud you're hiding in is even thicker now. You and the plane are totally covered.

Eventually Gallup Base calls off the search. You dash for the Turtalian border and freedom! Only when you land safely in Denver do you finally uncross your fingers.

The End

Matt carefully slides his hand away from the machine gun.

"Sit up. Slowly. And keep your hands in sight."

Everybody obeys. The voice is not friendly. You wonder how many there are besides him and how you were spotted.

Something moves through the dark, then a tall form steps into the moonlight outside your shallow cave.

It's not a soldier! You start to breathe a sigh of relief—then stop as you wonder who it could be.

The military briefing you got before you left Turtalia said there was nobody living in this area anymore. Doradan police used to come out here on "hunting trips" and shoot the natives for sport. "Maybe they didn't kill everybody," you think.

Turn to page 122.

"We'll have to set a time limit if we search," you say. "Let's say that if we don't find Haven in ten minutes, we give up. OK?"

"Good," Mimla agrees. "Let's go."

Shouldering Haven's bundle, you head out to look for him. Since you don't know what direction he went and there are no footprints, the three of you walk in a spiral pattern.

The terrain is hilly, and you can't see very far. There is no sign of Haven as the ten-minute limit approaches. Then you step over a rise and almost bump into him.

Unfortunately for all of you, Haven is in the company of a platoon of Doradan soldiers. For some reason, he is not tied up.

"Well, there you are," Haven says. "We've been looking all over for you."

"We?" you all say together.

"Allow me to introduce myself." He clicks his, heels together. "Haven Nightshade, Captain, Doradan Secret Police."

He bows slightly. "This time you will not escape."

The End

"Please, Julio," you say. "Use the special knock."

"What is it you want, *amigo*?"

"The special knock. You know it, Julio."

"Oh, *pardoneme*. I have forgotten it. *Por favor*, open! The curfew is starting!"

At that moment you hear the screech of jeep wheels and the angry shouts of soldiers. There is a burst of gunfire. Then the door flies open. Julio slumps to the ground behind it.

You are only slightly more lucky than your friend. The Doradan Secret Police have found you. You are about to find out what goes on behind the concrete walls across the street. Too bad.

The End

"Let's keep pushing through the mountains," you say.

"But—" Haven starts to object.

"I'm not going to Santa Fe," Mimla interrupts fiercely. "If there's still a chance for escape, we should take it."

"Well, let's go then," you say.

You all grab what you can out of the truck: blankets, food, canteens, rope. Matt covers the Blazer with some brush while the rest of you divide the supplies into bundles that can be carried.

Soon you're all ready. You head up to the top of the pass. From there it's easy to see the direction you need to go. You set off.

You don't get very far that day. By nightfall you're all exhausted from carrying the awkward loads in the high altitude, where there is less oxygen.

You'd like to make a campfire, but you're afraid of being spotted. As you sit in a circle eating, you tell each other stories of atrocities committed by the Doradan Secret Police. They fire you up for escaping, but not for a restful night's sleep.

The next day is like the one before. But then the weather turns bad, and blinding snow forces you to stop early. You take refuge in a cave and watch the snow come down.

Turn to page 120.

The cave provides a safe spot to light a fire, and at least you stay warm.

But the snow does not let up for three days. The trail becomes impassable. A short spell of good weather is followed by more snow. The four of you are trapped in the cave.

The food runs out. Too weak to walk, you finally starve to death. Haven is the last to go, because he turns cannibal. Eventually, though, he too succumbs, and it is . . .

The End

"We are escaping the Doradan Secret Police," you say.

The figure spits on the ground. "Those scum." He pauses. "I will answer your question now. We are Navajos. This is 'our' land, although Navajos do not believe that anyone can really own the land. Why are the Doradan scum after you?"

"We are—I mean were—political prisoners. We escaped from one of their jails." You want to tell him everything: the fact that you have top-secret information about invasion plans, who Mimla really is, everything. "I'd like to tell you more, but I can't. We have to get to Turtalia."

"I think I understand. Now it is your turn to ask a question."

You want to ask if he will help you escape, but you know his answer will only be "yes" or "no," and you need to know more. Then you have an idea.

"Why will you help us escape?"

You hear Matt and Mimla chuckle in the dark. Then the voice laughs, too.

"Good question. You are assuming we will help. Yes, we will. We will because we hate the Doradans as much as you do. Those scum who come to our villages and shoot our people for target practice, who talk of freedom and practice slavery. We will help because we know the woman who is traveling with you. We will help because we are Navajos."

Turn to page 85.

Matt breaks the silence. "We come in peace."

"And my mother is a horse," snorts the man holding the gun.

"Wait!" you shout. All eyes turn to you. Something about the man has triggered a thought.

"We are friends, not fiends," you say.

"Friends are always welcome," he replies.

"Could you spare some *frijoles* for a friend?"

The man grins back and lowers his gun.

"*Mi casa es su casa*," he says.

A Turtalian agent! You're saved! It's a good thing you remembered the passwords.

The agent, Miguel, and his compatriots squat in a circle around you.

"We have come down from Mesa Verde on an expedition," he explains. "We must continue, but I think I can spare Raphael, here"—he points to a skinny sixteen-year-old boy—"to help lead you north."

"Thank you," you respond. "You may have saved our lives—and Turtalia itself."

"Your journey will not be easy, *amigos*," Miguel warns, "but you will make it. Let me be the first to welcome you home."

The End

124

That night you are tired. The jerky you have for supper does not satisfy you, and you sleep fitfully.

Over breakfast the next day—more jerky—you discuss what to do.

"We're being forced to head towards Canyon de Chelly," Matt says.

"Maybe that's not so bad," you answer.

"Why?" asks Mimla.

"Because there are many good hiding places there. We can hole up for a few days. The searches will die down and then we can head the way we want to—toward home and freedom."

"Sounds good to me," says Matt.

You all shoulder your bundles and head off.

Late in the day you find yourself in different terrain. The canyons are steeper and deeper. There is more vegetation. You feel safe—except for a prickly sensation that you're being watched. You keep peering around, but see nobody. You decide not to tell the others about your hunch. You don't want to scare them.

That night you camp under a cedar tree. The animals make their usual night noises—then suddenly they stop. You hear footsteps approaching.

Turn to page 94.

GLOSSARY

Altimeter – A device always used in aircraft (but having many other uses) that measures the elevation of the aircraft above sea level or above the ground. It measures the height of land as in a mountain peak, or any designated geographical place. There are two types of altimeters. Pressure-activated altimeters are aneroid barometers that measure changes in atmospheric pressure to determine elevation. Radio altimeters measure the length of time it takes a radio signal to bounce back from land or sea.

Code – A message that uses substitute numbers, letters, symbols or meanings to mask the true content of the communication. Machines like the German WW11 Enigma machine encoded messages that were almost impossible to break. Computers can develop almost unbreakable codes.

Computer – An electronic machine that processes mathematical or logical operations at very high speed or that processes data or information.

Cumulus cloud – White popcorn-like clouds formed by rising air masses that are thermally unstable.

Curfew – A restriction or order commanding people to leave a specific area such as a city's streets or a certain building during certain hours. These orders are given by a governing body and are frequently used during times of war. Curfews are usually enforced by police or the military.

Dictatorship – A form of government with an absolute ruler who governs without the consent of the people. Adolf Hitler, Joseph Stalin, Mao Tse-Tung, and Genghis Kahn are all examples of dictators.

Motor glider – Gliders are motorless aircraft that depend upon the lift generated by their long, thin wings to achieve and sustain flight. They are extremely efficient. Gliders become airborne by either towing by a regular power aircraft or by some other form of launching such as a truck or winch. A motor glider combines the efficiency of glider design and the usefulness of a motor.

Secret police – A police force functioning under secrecy, usually without the legal restraints of a constitution. Secret police forces are often used by dictators and other repressive regimes to terrorize and control opposition.

Tachometer – A measuring device that displays or records the number of turns made by a rotating shaft. Cars, planes, and trucks use tachometers to gauge the output of their engines.

Transponder – A receiver-transmitter that becomes operational when receiving a signal. Transponders are used in planes for identification and location purposes.

Turbulence – Atmospheric turbulence is caused by the warming of air near the Earth's surface meeting cooler, upper air. Turbulence typically produces winds that are highly variable and that can become heavy and dangerous.

Variometer – Used in gliding, this instrument indicates the upward or downward movement of the glider.

CREDITS

Illustrator: Jason Millet. Since graduating from Chicago's American Academy of Art, Jason Millet has created artwork for companies ranging from Disney® to Absolut®. His client list includes Warner Brothers®, Major League Baseball®, the Chicago Bulls® and Hallmark®, among many others. This is his first *Choose Your Own Adventure*® book.

Cover Artist: Sittisan Sundaravej (Quan). Sittisan is a resident of Bangkok, Thailand and an old fan of *Choose Your Own Adventure*. He attended The University of the Arts in Philadelphia, where he received his BSC in architecture and a BFA for animation. He has been a 2D and 3D animation director for productions in Asia and the United States and is a freelance illustrator.

Cover Artist: Kriangsak Thongmoon (Tao). Kriangsak is a graphic artist living in Thailand. After attending Srinakarinwiroj Prasarnmitr University in Bangkok, Kriangsak made a career illustrating for various well-known publications in Thailand before switching his concentrations to 3D modeling and computer animation. However, his love for drawing and sketching still keeps him coming back to non-computer generated illustrations.

This book was brought to life by a great group of people:

Shannon Gilligan, Publisher
Gordon Troy, General Counsel
Jason Gellar, Sales Director
Melissa Bounty, Senior Editor
Stacey Boyd, Designer

Thanks to everyone involved!

Buy the paperback version of this title and others at www.cyoa.com.

ABOUT THE AUTHOR

R. A. MONTGOMERY has hiked in the Himalayas, climbed mountains in Europe, scuba-dived in Central America, and worked in Africa. He lives in France in the winter, travels frequently to Asia, and calls Vermont home. Montgomery graduated from Williams College and attended graduate school at Yale University and NYU. His interests include macro-economics, geo-politics, mythology, history, mystery novels, and music. He has two grown sons, a daughter-in-law, and two grand-daughters. His wife, Shannon Gilligan, is an author and noted interactive game designer. Montgomery feels that the new generation of people under 15 is the most important asset in our world.

For games, activities and other fun stuff, or to write to R. A. Montgomery, visit us online at CYOA.com